Amelia Bedelia

Amelia Bedelia

by Peggy Parish

pictures by Fritz Siebel

HarperCollinsPublishers

 Printed in the United States of America. For information address HarperCollins Children's Books, a division of HarperCollins Publishers, 10 East 53rd Street, New York, NY 10022. www.harperchildrens.com

Library of Congress Cataloging-in-Publication Data
Parish, Peggy.
Amelia Bedelia / by Peggy Parish ; pictures by Fritz Siebel. — New ed.
p. cm. — (An I can read book)
Summary: A literal-minded housekeeper causes a ruckus in the household when she attempts to make sense of some instructions.
ISBN-10: 0-06-020186-X (trade bdg.) — ISBN-13: 978-0-06-020186-9 (trade bdg.)
ISBN-10: 0-06-020187-8 (lib. bdg.) — ISBN-13: 978-0-06-020187-6 (lib. bdg.)
ISBN-10: 0-06-444155-5 (pbk.) — ISBN-13: 978-0-06-444155-1 (pbk.)
[1. Humorous stories.] I. Siebel, Fritz, ill. II. Title. III. Series.
PZ7.P219Am 1992 91-10163
[E]—dc20 CIP
AC

❖

14 15 16 17 18 LP/WOR 20 19 18 17

For Debbie, John Grier,
Walter, and Michael Dinkins

“Oh, Amelia Bedelia,
your first day of work,
and I can’t be here.
But I made a list for you.
You do just what the list says,”
said Mrs. Rogers.
Mrs. Rogers got into the car
with Mr. Rogers.
They drove away.

"My, what nice folks.
I'm going to like working here,"
said Amelia Bedelia.

Change the towels in green
Dust the furniture.
comes in.
a steak and a chicken.
Please trim the fat before you
put the steak in the icebox.
And please dress the chicken.

Amelia Bedelia went inside.
"Such a grand house.
These must be rich folks.
But I must get to work.
Here I stand just looking.
And me with a whole list
of things to do."
Amelia Bedelia stood there
a minute longer.
"I think I'll make
a surprise for them.
I'll make lemon-meringue pie.
I do make good pies."

So Amelia Bedelia went
into the kitchen.
She put a little of this
and a pinch of that
into a bowl.
She mixed and she rolled.

Soon her pie was ready
to go into the oven.
“There,” said Amelia Bedelia.
“That’s done.”

"Now let's see what this list says."

Amelia Bedelia read,

Change the towels in the green bathroom.

Amelia Bedelia found
the green bathroom.
"Those towels are very nice.
Why change them?" she thought.

Then Amelia Bedelia remembered
what Mrs. Rogers had said.
She must do just what
the list told her.
"Well, all right,"
said Amelia Bedelia.
Amelia Bedelia got some scissors.
She snipped a little here
and a little there.
And she changed those towels.

"There," said Amelia Bedelia.

She looked at her list again.

Dust the furniture.

"Did you ever hear tell

of such a silly thing.

At my house we undust the furniture.

But to each his own way."

Amelia Bedelia took

one last look at the bathroom.

She saw a big box with the words

Dusting Powder on it.

"Well, look at that.
A special powder to dust with!"
exclaimed Amelia Bedelia.
So Amelia Bedelia
dusted the furniture.
"That should be dusty enough.
My, how nice it smells."

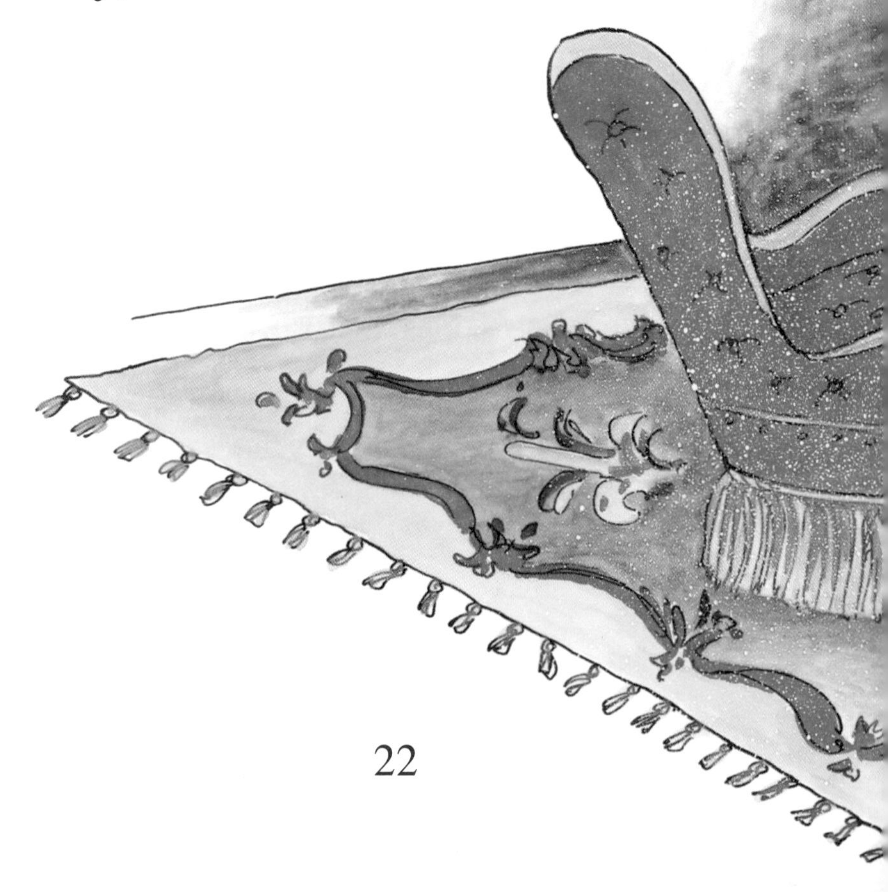

Draw the drapes when the sun comes in.

read Amelia Bedelia.
She looked up.
The sun was coming in.
Amelia Bedelia looked
at the list again.
"Draw the drapes?
That's what it says.
I'm not much
of a hand at drawing,
but I'll try."

So Amelia Bedelia sat right down
and she drew those drapes.

Amelia Bedelia
marked off
about the drapes.
"Now what?"

Put the lights out when you finish in the living room.

Amelia Bedelia
thought about this a minute.
She switched off the lights.
Then she carefully
unscrewed each bulb.

And Amelia Bedelia
put the lights out.
“So those things need
to be aired out, too.
Just like pillows and babies.
Oh, I do have a lot to learn.”

“My pie!” exclaimed Amelia Bedelia.

She hurried to the kitchen.

“Just right,” she said.

She took the pie out of the oven

and put it on the table to cool.

Then she looked at the list.

Measure two cups of rice.

"That's next," said Amelia Bedelia.

Amelia Bedelia found two cups.

She filled them with rice.

And Amelia Bedelia
measured that rice.

Amelia Bedelia laughed.
"These folks
do want me to do funny things."
Then she poured the rice
back into the container.

The meat market will deliver a steak and a chicken.

Please trim the fat before you put the steak in the icebox.

And please dress the chicken.

When the meat arrived,

Amelia Bedelia opened the bag.

She looked at the steak

for a long time.

"Yes," she said.

"That will do nicely."

Amelia Bedelia got some lace
and bits of ribbon.
And Amelia Bedelia
trimmed that fat
before she put
the steak in the icebox.

“Now I must dress the chicken.
I wonder if she wants
a he chicken or a she chicken?”
said Amelia Bedelia.
Amelia Bedelia went right to work.
Soon the chicken was finished.

Amelia Bedelia heard the door open.

"The folks are back," she said.

She rushed out to meet them.

“Amelia Bedelia,
why are all the light bulbs outside?”
asked Mr. Rogers.

"The list just said

to put the lights out,"

said Amelia Bedelia.

"It didn't say to bring them back in.

Oh, I do hope

they didn't get aired too long."

“Amelia Bedelia,

the sun will fade the furniture.

I asked you to draw the drapes,”

said Mrs. Rogers.

“I did! I did! See,”

said Amelia Bedelia.

She held up her picture.

Then Mrs. Rogers saw the furniture.

"The furniture!" she cried.

"Did I dust it well enough?"
asked Amelia Bedelia.
"That's such nice dusting powder."

Mr. Rogers went to wash his hands.

"I say," he called.

"These are very unusual towels."

Mrs. Rogers dashed into the bathroom.

"Oh, my best towels," she said.

"Didn't I change them enough?"

asked Amelia Bedelia.

Mrs. Rogers went to the kitchen.

"I'll cook the dinner.

Where is the rice

I asked you to measure?"

"I put it back in the container.
But I remember—
it measured four and a half inches,"
said Amelia Bedelia.

"Was the meat delivered?"
asked Mrs. Rogers.
"Yes," said Amelia Bedelia.
"I trimmed the fat just like you said.
It does look nice."
Mrs. Rogers rushed to the icebox.
She opened it.
"Lace! Ribbons!
Oh, dear!" said Mrs. Rogers.

MILK
FISH

"The chicken—you dressed
the chicken?"
asked Mrs. Rogers.
"Yes, and I found the nicest box
to put him in,"
said Amelia Bedelia.
"Box!" exclaimed Mrs. Rogers.
Mrs. Rogers hurried over to the box.
She lifted the lid.
There lay the chicken.
And he was just as dressed
as he could be.

Mrs. Rogers was angry.

She was very angry.

She opened her mouth.

Mrs. Rogers meant

to tell Amelia Bedelia

she was fired.

But before she could

get the words out,

Mr. Rogers put something

in her mouth.

It was so good

Mrs. Rogers forgot about being angry.

"Lemon-meringue pie!"
she exclaimed.
"I made it to surprise you,"
said Amelia Bedelia happily.
So right then and there
Mr. and Mrs. Rogers decided
that Amelia Bedelia must stay.
And so she did.
Mrs. Rogers learned to say
undust the furniture,
unlight the lights,
close the drapes,
and things like that.

Mr. Rogers didn’t care
if Amelia Bedelia
trimmed all
of his steaks with lace.

All he cared about
was having her there
to make lemon-meringue pie.